Tryouts!

I could feel Miss Elise's eyes on me.

I moved my feet; I did the port de bras. I felt as if my legs were marshmallows, my arms were sticks.

I closed my eyes and listened to the music. I thought of the Juliet dancer and tried to believe in myself. "Breathe ballet," I whispered.

And then it was over. I walked home with Miss Elise. She talked about Joy's grace, Karen's good posture. She talked about Stephanie's smile, and how well I was coming along.

But the one thing she didn't say was who she was going to choose.

And that's the only thing I really wanted to hear.

OTHER CHAPTER BOOKS FROM PUFFIN

BALLET SLIPPERS™

6

Rosie's Big City Ballet

by Patricia Reilly Giff

illustrated by Julie Durrell

PUFFIN BOOKS

Love to Ali O',
the girl in the pink dress

PUFFIN BOOKS
Published by the Penguin Group
Penguin Putnam Books for Young Readers,
345 Hudson Street, New York, New York 10014, U.S.A.
Penguin Books Ltd, 27 Wrights Lane, London W8 5TZ, England
Penguin Books Australia Ltd, Ringwood, Victoria, Australia
Penguin Books Canada Ltd, 10 Alcorn Avenue, Toronto, Ontario, Canada M4V 3B2
Penguin Books (N.Z.) Ltd, 182-190 Wairau Road, Auckland 10, New Zealand

Penguin Books Ltd, Registered Offices: Harmondsworth, Middlesex, England

First published in the United States of America by Viking,
a member of Penguin Putnam Inc., 1998
Published by Puffin Books,
a member of Penguin Putnam Books for Young Readers, 1999

7 9 10 8 6

THE LIBRARY OF CONGRESS HAS CATALOGED THE VIKING EDITION AS FOLLOWS:
Giff, Patricia Reilly.
Rosie's big city ballet / by Patricia Reilly Giff; illustrated by Julie Durrell.
p. cm.—(Ballet slippers; 6)
Summary: When Rosie sets her heart on being selected for a part in Miss
Déirdre's summer ballet performance, she has no idea that she may
be chosen for something even better.
ISBN 0-670-87792-1
[1. Ballet—Fiction. 2. Competition (Psychology) —Fiction.]
I. Durrell, Julie, ill. II. Title. III. Series: Giff, Patricia Reilly. Ballet slippers; 6.
PZ7.G3626Rj 1998 [Fic]—dc21 97-29767 CIP AC

Puffin Books ISBN 0-14-130167-8

Printed in the United States of America

RL: 2.5

Chapter 1

It was a dream. I was standing in back of a soft velvet curtain...standing so still I felt almost invisible.

A hundred things were going on around me and I was watching all of them. I was shivering because I was so excited.

Workers had put a barre in the center of the stage. Some of the dancers were warming up.

Just then, Amy Stetson, my fourteen-year-old ballerina friend, grabbed my hand. I jumped. It wasn't a dream after all. I was in the big city to see the ballet, the story of Romeo and Juliet.

Amy was still wearing old purple sweats and red leg warmers. "Come on, Rosie," she said. "I want you to see the rest."

She pulled me across the stage. A man was tee-tering on the top of a ladder, fiddling with the lights.

"The computer takes care of most of the light-ing," Amy told me. "But the electrician checks to see that everything is perfect."

She waved her hand. "There's where I'll be. A dancer in the ball scene, part of the *corps de ballet*."

I nodded. I knew what the *corps de ballet* meant. It was a large group who danced together. Miss Deirdre had told us that a million times.

Amy pointed to a pair of huge white columns at the sides of the stage. "Two girls will stand there with baskets of flowers," she said, and shook her head. "No, just one girl until we can find a new one. The other girl moved away."

"Fifteen minutes," the stage manager called.

Amy drew in her breath. "Not much time." She led me down a hallway to the changing rooms. They were packed with dancers. The dancers were putting on tutus, combing their hair, sewing ribbons on their slippers.

Then I saw a beautiful dancer at a table. Her hair was pulled back into a tight bun. She was smearing white makeup over her face.

She reached out and gave my nose a quick dab with the sponge. "First time?" she asked.

I took a breath. I wanted to tell her I had seen ballet before. It wasn't like this, though, not in the city with a huge stage and a million seats outside.

I wanted to tell her my grandmother had been a ballerina.

I wanted to tell her that Amy was my friend. I wanted to say that Amy was a real ballerina, and that she had brought me to watch.

But the dancer wasn't paying attention. She was leaning into the mirror, reaching for false eyelashes. Jars and tubes of makeup were spread out in front of her.

I gave it a try. "I'm going to be a ballerina," I told her. Then I couldn't believe I had said that aloud.

She turned back to look at me. "Do you prac-

tice?" she asked. "Every single day, day in, day out, even when you don't feel like practicing?"

I half nodded, thinking that sometimes I skipped, that I wasn't nearly as good as I wanted to be. "Well…"

The dancer waved her hand. "I thought so." Now she was really looking at me, blinking a little. She had one false eyelash on her eye. The other one was in her hand, looking like a long, black caterpillar.

I could hear the stage manager calling, "Five minutes."

Amy grabbed my hand again. "I have to get ready," she said. "Good thing I'm not on stage until later…until the ball scene."

But the dancer reached out with one finger and touched my shoulder. "Almost no one turns out to be a dancer," she said. "A real dancer."

"I'm going to try…." I began. I knew she didn't believe me. I almost didn't believe it myself.

Amy was trying to pull me out into the hallway again. "We have to hurry," she said. "I have to finish dressing. I have to get you out in front."

The dancer was still talking. "What's your name, girl in the pink dress?"

"Rosie," I said. "Rosaleen O'Meara."

"Take this," she said.

I let go of Amy's hand and reached for the small wooden puppet she held out to me.

"It's Juliet," she told me. "If you ever want to dance the part of Juliet, you'll have to practice."

I nodded once more. "I'll put her in my bedroom. I'll practice every day."

She smiled. "I'm the understudy for the part of Juliet. But one day I'll have the part. I know it. Believing in yourself is the most important part of all."

Now Amy was dragging me away. We went across the stage again, down a tiny flight of stairs, up another flight, and out a door.

In back of me, I could hear the stage manager calling again, "Beginners, please, onstage."

In the aisle, a woman in a black dress was giving out programs.

"Would you put Rosie in her seat, please?" Amy asked, waving my ticket.

By the time I turned around to wish her luck, she had disappeared into the doorway again. The woman in black rushed me up another set of stairs to the balcony. She waved a small flashlight to show me where to sit.

And in another moment, I was leaning over the railing. I watched people taking their seats and the orchestra warming up in front of us.

I held on to the tiny wooden puppet and ran my fingers over her smiling face. She had long, dark painted eyelashes. She almost looked like the dancer who had given her to me.

Suddenly the lights in the huge chandeliers dimmed. Everyone was still.

I was there to see *Romeo and Juliet*. I was there to see Amy in the *corps de ballet*.

The ballet began. I felt as if I had stepped into a

new world. I saw the dancers, leaping and twirling, sometimes alone, sometimes with partners. Later I caught a glimpse of Amy. She was dancing at the ball wearing a pale blue tutu. And near her, in front of one of the columns was a girl with a basket of white flowers.

By the time it was over, by the time Amy's father had come to take us home, I was wishing I'd be Juliet someday.

I wondered if I ever could. The Juliet dancer said you had to believe. I didn't know if I could really do that. I crossed my fingers.

Chapter 2

It was two days later. I was still thinking about the big city ballet, still humming a little of the music. And there was something else. Something special. But right now, my best friend Murphy was waiting for me.

"Want to come, Jake?" I snapped my fingers at the cat.

I *bouréed* across the street, over the curb and around a puddle, feeling good, feeling great. I *pirouetted* into Tommy Murphy's yard.

Jake *pirouetted* along in back of me.

It was the first day of spring ... and it felt like spring. The sun was warm on my head, and the

daffodils were open. I felt the syrup of happiness, as my teacher called it, spreading around in my chest.

I stepped around the bare spot where Murph and I had planted sunflowers under his itchy-ball tree. Who knew if they'd ever grow?

And that's where Murph was right now: halfway up the trunk of the itchy-ball tree. He was hanging onto a branch with one hand.

In two jumps, Jake was up next to him, head turned, watching him.

"You're going to end up killing yourself," I said. "Even Jake thinks you're crazy."

Murph grinned down at me. "Don't be silly. It's not that far. I could jump right from here."

I kept going, not listening. "And just when I have the best news in the world."

He didn't answer. He swayed back and forth, looking up at the sky and squinting.

That's Murph.

"You'll go blind if you look at the sun," I said. "Grandpa told me."

Murph closed one eye.

"Anyway," I said, "someone is coming to see our ballet class at Dance with Miss Deirdre this spring. Someone special."

Murph let go of the branch and dropped to the ground. "It's possible," he said.

"It's definite," I told him. "She's an artistic director, very important. That's the person who decides which ballet to do. She even chooses the dancers."

Murph was walking around the tree.

"Her name is Miss Elise."

He shook his head. "If I can just get wood…" He broke off and walked around the tree trunk. "You can hold…that is if you want…"

I knew he wasn't listening. He was thinking of something else. I might as well be talking to myself.

I said it anyway. "She's going to choose someone to play a part in her summer ballet. It will be right here in Miss Deirdre's studio. Right here in

Lynfield." I rushed on. "Grown-ups, of course. But one girl from the class. Just one."

"A terrific tree house," Murph said. "I know we can do it."

"Maybe she'll even choose me." Now I really was talking to myself. I'd never say that aloud.

The sun slid behind a cloud and it wasn't as warm as it had been a minute ago. How could I think she'd choose me? I wasn't the best. There were at least three other girls who were as good as I was. And Joy Mead was better.

Murph was looking at me hard. I jumped. For a moment I wondered if I had said all this aloud.

But he was leaning forward. His lips were still chapped from the winter. His big flat ears were a little red from the wind.

Tommy Murphy was the best friend I ever had in my life. He had a great face, especially when he smiled.

And he was smiling now. "I really want to do this tree house," he said. "We can spend all summer in it, watching the world. I'll keep an eye on the birds, and study the bugs on the branches, the leaves…"

Summer. I thought of the Juliet dancer I had met, and the puppet hanging on my doorknob.

I was going to practice and practice … even though the Juliet dancer didn't believe me.

Across the street, I could hear Grandpa whistling "Rakes of Mallow." "Da-da-dum-dum-dum-dum-dum-dum-da-da-da-da."

It was his signal to me, time for dinner. Monday night, chili with brown bread and tortilla chips. I loved it.

Murphy was still staring at me. "Want to help?"

Sure I did. I could practice ballet every night. "Don't worry," I told him. "I will."

I *pirouetted* across the street and *bouréed* around to the back of the house. I could see Amy Stetson across the way. She was practicing ballet on her back porch.

I stopped to watch her. She was holding onto

14

the back of a high chair, working on *pliés*. She was doing the same movements over and over. Her feet were in first position. She bent her knees as far as she could without raising her heels. Then she straightened her legs.

A moment later she started over again.

She had told me about that the other night. "Do each movement a million times, Rosie. Then it'll be perfect."

That's just what I was going to do ... as soon as I got a minute.

I went up the steps and held the door open for Jake before I went into the kitchen. My little brother Andrew was sitting there drawing, making great scribble-scrabble lines.

"It's a card," he told me.

Grandpa rolled his eyes at me.

"What does it say?" I swooped down to give him a quick hug.

"What do you think it says?" he asked.

"Uhm ..." Grandpa was mouthing something at me. *Well?* Was it *well?*

I shut my eyes. I didn't know anyone who was sick. "A get-well card?"

Andrew shook his head. Brown bread crumbs and butter circled his mouth.

"How about…" I looked at Grandpa again.

He really was saying *well.*

"I give up, Andrew." I reached across him for a piece of bread.

"That's the surprise, Rosie," he said. "It's a *Welcome to See Us* card."

"Nice." I slid onto my chair. My mother and father had gone to the city, so it was just the three of us for dinner.

"Very nice," Andrew said. "But remember…" He held up a buttery finger. "You can't sleep in your bed, you can't stay in your room. Company's coming."

"Not Aunt Cleo…" I began. I could see Murph out the window. He was climbing the itchy-ball tree again.

Then I looked back. Grandpa was grinning. "The artistic director has to stay somewhere."

Miss Elise, here, in my house, my kitchen, my room.

I thought of trying out for her summer ballet.

I couldn't swallow the brown bread. I couldn't even breathe.

Chapter 3

It was Tuesday afternoon. I had about two minutes to spare before ballet lessons.

I had pulled up the rug in front of my bed, and was doing *pliés* like Amy Stetson, in my socks on the bare wood floor.

Over my bed was a picture of my grandmother Genevieve, her leg raised in a *grand battement.* She was wearing a white net tutu, with feathers covering her hair. She was absolutely beautiful.

Genevieve had been a famous ballerina, and in my mind, I was dancing for her. I always did that, making believe she was right there watching me and smiling.

And I talked to her. I told her about Miss Elise.

I told her about the tryouts. "It's a tiny part, the teeniest tiniest bit of a dance."

I was out of breath. I looked over to my little wooden Juliet. "Could you see me? A real dancer?"

"Roooosssssie!"

It was Karen Cooper shouting at the top of her lungs.

I took a quick look out the window. Karen was galloping along on Murphy's side of the street, coming toward me.

I pushed up the window. "Coming," I shouted down to her.

I grabbed my ballet bag, took the stairs two at a time, and called back to Grandpa, "I'm on my way. See you later."

I hopped over Jake and out the door.

Karen was waiting for me, twirling around, eyes closed, swinging her ballet bag in the air. "Ride 'em, cowboy," she was yelling.

"Don't let go of that." I ducked as the bag sailed past me.

Karen opened her eyes. "Oops, sorry. I was thinking about being in a rodeo."

We hurried down the street, heading for Scranton Avenue and Dance with Miss Deirdre. Murph was on his way back from the hardware store. A couple of pieces of wood were slung over one shoulder, and a bag of stuff, nails or screws I guessed, was slung over the other.

"Where are you going?" he asked, and dropped the whole mess down in front of him. "I thought you promised to work with me on—" he began.

"It's Tuesday," I said. "Ballet lessons this afternoon, switched from Monday."

I could see his shoulders slump. He was doing it on purpose. It was mime, acting out feelings without words. Miss Deirdre had taught us that in ballet class, and I had taught Murph one day last winter.

I waved, and Karen and I crossed the street. Karen was neighing every few seconds. She was dying for a horse, dying to take riding lessons.

Too bad there probably wasn't a horse within fifty miles of Lynfield.

Five minutes later, we turned in at the alley in back of the studio. We passed Gee-Gee's Toys and Delano's Delicious Chocolates.

And then we were there, opening the door under the Dance with Miss Deirdre sign and racing down the stairs.

Miss Serena was at the piano already, playing wonderful thumping notes. I tried a *grand plié* on the bottom step, and Stephanie Witt, who was clattering down the stairs, landed on top of me.

We crashed onto the floor in a heap.

I knew my knee was skinned, and one elbow. I tried not to let Stephanie know she felt like an elephant. After all, it was my fault. "Sorry," I tried to say.

We lay there for another second, until I finally told her I was going to stop breathing.

Miss Deirdre was frowning at both of us. She

looked up at the clock. "One minute to four," she said. "We're ready to begin."

In the blink of an eye, I had pulled off my sneakers, put on my good-luck pink ballet slippers, and stuffed my jacket behind my back in the corner.

I sank down on the mat in the middle of the room and blew on my sore knee while we waited for Karen and Stephanie.

"Now . . ." Miss Deirdre said.

Miss Serena played a *ta-da*.

"We have to think about . . ." Miss Deirdre began.

"The artistic director," everyone in the class said at once.

Miss Deirdre talked about how hard we had to practice. Miss Elise would watch our work at the barre. Then each of us would do a dance with a *glissade derrière*, a *changement*, a couple of *soutenu*, and a *pas de chat* or two.

"Whew," said Stephanie.

"Whew," I said, too, but under my breath.

"And for the next three weeks," said Miss Deirdre, her hands stretched out in front of her, "*Breathe ballet.*"

I nodded. That's exactly what I was going to do. Next to me, Karen and Stephanie and Joy and everyone else were nodding, too.

Then we started warm-ups at the barre, but Murph's face kept popping into my head. Murph waiting for me to help.

First position: heels together, feet and legs to the sides. I could hear Miss Deirdre calling, "No marshmallow legs, please."

Murph was probably dragging all those pieces of wood into his yard. Maybe he had even gone back to the store for more. He wouldn't have one cent of his birthday money left.

Second position: feet apart and turned out, Third: heel of one foot against the middle of the other.

Murph really couldn't lift the boards up to the tree branch alone.

Open fourth: foot forward from first position,

and ... "Keep smiling, Rosie," Miss Deirdre was saying. "Otherwise the audience will go home."

And then I was working as hard as I could, forgetting about Murph and the tree house and thinking only about ballet.

Breathing ballet.

Chapter 4

It was almost dark when I reached our street. A couple of lights were on, and it was getting cold.

It didn't feel like spring. It felt like January again. I pulled up my collar and raced for home.

I took a quick look across at Murph's house. The sunflowers we had planted were light green specks under the itchy-ball tree. Poor things would probably freeze to death.

Murph's dog, Homer, was sitting at the window, but Murph was probably having dinner. I could see one board teetering on a branch. Pieces of wood were spread out under the tree, and Mr. Murphy's toolbox was on the path.

Mr. Murphy would have a fit if it rained on

his hammer and screwdriver.

Inside, my mother was walking around the kitchen in her bare feet. She was touching the walls with her fingertips.

"Listen, Rosie," she said, giving me a quick kiss. "We have to wash down the walls, we have to paint. We certainly have to do something about the curtain in the dining room."

Andrew poked his head out from under the kitchen table. "It's for the company, Rosie," he said. "This house is okay for regular people. It's a mess for that lady-what's-her-name."

"The artistic director? Elise." I looked at Grandpa. "Can I help? I love to paint."

"Red," said Andrew. "It's my favorite color in the whole world."

Grandpa held up one hand. "Red is a little strong, Andrew my boy. And Rosie, you have to practice ballet, right?" He ran his hand over his face, thinking. "I'll paint it a nice soft…"

"Yellow, I think," said my mother.

"That's the ticket," said Grandpa.

"Right," said my father, nodding. "I'll give you a hand."

I sat down at the table. I could smell the chicken fingers frying in the skillet.

And then I thought about my bedroom. Stuff all over the place, ballet pictures half falling off the wall because the tape was old, my drawers so stuffed with junk I could hardly open them. Impossible!

I ate the chicken, the string beans, and a bite of the tomato salad to make my mother happy. The whole time, everyone was talking about Miss Elise, the artistic director, and cleaning the house.

After I finished the raspberry Jell-O, I went upstairs with Andrew and Jake the cat to take a look at my bedroom.

But first I stopped on the landing for a quick run-through of the five positions. I had to remember: the most important thing was ballet.

Breathe ballet.

Andrew watched me. "Nice feet wiggling," he said.

"Think so?" I asked, feeling the syrup of happiness in my chest. "I hope Miss Elise thinks so, too."

A moment later, we stood in my doorway. "Worse than my room." Andrew sounded happy about it. "Much worse." He grinned up at me. "Terrible. Like a garbage can."

I had to laugh. I always had to laugh at Andrew. I gave the top of his head a quick kiss. Then I *bouréed* across the room, trying to be graceful. I slid past the window and landed on the bed.

The streetlights were on, and I could see Murph. He was out there alone, trying to lift a board onto a tree branch.

I closed my eyes.

I wasn't going to think about Murph.

I wasn't going to think about my messy bedroom.

I was going to start from the very beginning of ballet and work on everything I'd learned. The five positions for my feet, and for my arms.

And don't forget the rest of it, I told myself.

Glissade derrière, and *changement*, and … What were the others? Yes. *Soutenu* and *pas de chat*.

Andrew had wandered away. I could hear him down the hall. He was looking at his own bedroom.

"Very nice, Andrew," he was saying. "Trains on the floor, and knights on the table. Just the way it should be."

I rolled up the rug and shoved it under the bed. I was ready to begin.

I went through the positions, back straight as an ironing board. I was watching Murph out of the corner of my eye.

I started with my arms … at my sides in first position, and then up a bit for *demi-seconde*.

I was feeling good. This was just what Amy Stetson was probably doing next door.

Across the street was a loud clatter. Murph had dropped the board. It had crashed onto the cement path below.

I raised my arms out at shoulder level for second position.…

Murph was my best friend.

He'd never get that tree house finished without me.

But what about *port de bras?* I asked myself. I had to get my arm exercises down pat. "Make your arms like palm trees waving gracefully," Miss Deirdre always said. "Not like a pair of sticks."

I made myself work another fifteen minutes. Then I went downstairs and into the kitchen. Grandpa and my mother and father were still at the table.

"Is it all right if I go out?" I asked.

My mother raised her eyebrows.

"Just across the street," I said. "Just for a few minutes. Just to help Murph. I'll be back in…"

I was still talking as I raced out the door and across the street.

"Don't worry, Murph," I yelled. "I'm on my way."

Chapter 5

I wasn't looking where I was going. Head down, I raced up our driveway and—

"Oof," I said as I collided with Amy Stetson.

Both of us blinked. "Sorry," I told her, and "Why aren't you doing ballet?"

She grinned at me. "Actually, I am. I'm exercising, strengthening my legs." The whole time, she was running in place, raising her feet, her arms outstretched and fingers pointed.

I stopped on one foot, pointing the other one in back of me. I hoped she was noticing.

And she was. "I told the Juliet dancer how hard you're working," she said. She circled around a tree and turned the corner.

Murph was across the street, waiting for me. I

knew he was glad to see me, but he was frowning, pretending he didn't care.

He put some nails out on a board. "As long as you're here," he said, "you can hand stuff up to me."

"Sure," I told him, running in place like Amy, my arms over my head, *en haut,* in fifth position, making a picture frame, as Miss Deirdre would say.

"If you can stop hopping around," he said.

He began to climb, one hand over the other, halfway up the itchy-ball tree. It was darker now, and getting cold. The bare branches were beginning to whip around in the wind.

I shivered and blew on my fingers to warm them. "Maybe we should work on this tomorrow," I called up.

He didn't answer. Once Murph had made up his mind, there was no changing it.

But there was another thing. I knew what Murph was thinking. He could picture this tree

house in his mind. It would be all painted up and perfect. He'd be lying there, the sun warm on his head, and he'd be looking up at the clouds, or maybe the leaves.

He thought about stuff like that the way I thought about being a ballerina. I could see myself on the stage in the big city. I was wearing a white tulle tutu with feathers in my hair.

Murph snapped his fingers at me.

"Just keep doing that," I said, trying to snap my fingers back at him, "and you'll be out of the tree and on the—"

I didn't get to finish.

He stopped snapping and started pointing at the pieces of wood and sticks.

"This one?" I began to pull one end of a board. It was rough and heavy.

I staggered over to the trunk of the tree and began to pass it up.

Murph was reaching, reaching.

I stood high up on tiptoes, trying to get the

board in a spot so he could grab it. "Careful," I said.

I hated to fool around with anything high up. I knew I could never climb up to that tree house, even though Grandpa agreed with Murph. "It's only a step and a hop or two," he had said last night.

Murph touched the board with the tips of his fingers.

I tried to hold it steady, and slowly, he dragged it toward him, up and over the branch.

And then I waited forever while he hammered a thousand nails into the board and the tree.

I thought about seeing *Romeo and Juliet* the other night. The two of them meeting at a ball, falling in love, and their families saying they couldn't get married.

It was such a sad story, both of them dying rather than give each other up. I'd never do that in a million years, I was thinking.

And that's when Murph hit his thumb with

the hammer. "Yeow!" he yelled at the top of his lungs.

The hammer came crashing down. So did the board.

I jumped out of the way just in time to see Murph trying to get his balance, trying to hold on. Then, almost in slow motion, he began to fall.

Chapter 6

The next morning, I woke with the sun in patches on my bed. I was still thinking about Murph, knowing part of it was my fault. If I had been paying attention, the whole thing might not have happened.

I went downstairs for breakfast, feeling as if somehow I would be in trouble with everyone.

But no one knew it had been my fault, too.

"I'd hate not to go to school today like Tommy Murphy," Andrew was saying. "We're making pictures with nuts all over them. You can put mine in your room, Rosie. The ballerina will love it."

"I'll love it, too," I told him.

My mother had a pencil in her hand. "I'll make

Jell-O for Tommy," she said. "Orange. Right after work. Just the thing for a sprained ankle."

She made a doodle face on her paper. "But then we have to work on this house for the ballerina."

"Listen," I said. "I have to breathe ballet today."

"Listen," my mother said, smiling at me. "You have to breathe the house. Take some of the old games out of the family room. Put them in the cellar. We should have done that years ago."

"But I'll never be picked if I don't practice," I said. "Joy is working every day. She's the best. Really. And even Karen and Stephanie . . ." I stopped. I wanted to say that we'd never get the house fixed in time. But my mother was shaking her head.

"It won't take that long," she said. "You'll see."

"It's going to look like a castle," Andrew said. "The one with the prince in it."

I laughed. "You're the prince, Andrew," I said.

He thought about it. "Yes," he said.

I went off to school trying to figure it all out. How to stop in and see Murph. How to help with the house. Homework. How to work in enough time for ballet. How to breathe ballet. I had to do it.

I turned in at the schoolyard gate. All the kids from my ballet class were talking about Miss Elise coming and how lucky I was she was staying at our house.

I was beginning to realize that I would have been luckier if she had stayed somewhere else.

"I can feel the difference," Joy was saying. "My legs are stronger, and my feet. I'm working every day."

Stephanie was nodding. "Yes."

Stephanie, a neat kid, a horrible dancer. But I could see she was feeling surer of herself. So maybe she really was better than before.

I swallowed. I didn't feel any better, not one bit. And the truth was I didn't want anyone else to feel better.

That was mean, I knew it.

But I wanted to be the one who was picked.

I had never wanted anything more.

The bell rang, then. It was time to go inside.

It was strange not to see Murphy in his seat. Really strange to think of him home with his foot up, looking out the window or something.

And something else. Murph wanted that tree house as much as I wanted the ballet. It was part of his dream to be a scientist someday.

A thought came into my head. A thought about the tree house.

It kept popping up all day, between Math and Social Studies, after lunch, and during recess.

Murphy really couldn't build the house now, not with a sprained ankle. My mother had said it would be days before he could hop around all over the place the way he usually did.

I was afraid of climbing the tree, so I certainly couldn't do it for him.

I had to breathe ballet.

Poor Murph.

The thought came again. Suppose I got my courage up? Suppose somehow I could climb the tree and pull the rest of the boards up? Suppose I could nail them down? Murph would tell me how.

Suppose somehow I could get up an hour earlier? Practice ballet. Clean my room.

Suppose.

I sighed.

I knew I had to try.

Chapter 7

This was some Saturday, I thought to myself, smiling. It was the beginning of spring break. Andrew and I had made forty trips down to the basement. We'd taken every bit of junk out of the family room.

We were both full of dust. Andrew even had a cobweb in his hair.

My mother was in my room now, changing sheets, puffing up pillows. My father was putting the ladder away, and Grandpa was touching up the last bit of molding with a paintbrush dipped in yellow. Somehow the old blue paint from underneath made the new paint look almost green.

"It wasn't the way I thought it would be," my

mother said, stepping back. "But I like it. I really do."

I did, too. Miss Elise was arriving tonight, and I had to say the house looked great. Andrew was right. It almost looked like a castle.

That's what my mother said, too. "See, Rosie, anything is possible. No one could guess what a mess this place was."

A few minutes later, I could hear Andrew in the tub. I knew he'd be floating around with his sailboats, splashing all over the place.

I was still a mess, with dirt on my face and my neck, and a ripped shirt. But I had a lot to do.

No bath for me yet.

Glissade derrière. Changement. Soutenu. Pas de chat. Twice each.

Then I headed across the street. I could see Murph upstairs in his bedroom. He was leaning over, hanging onto the windowsill, waiting for me.

We had talked the whole thing over last night. "You can do it, Rosie," he said when he heard my plan. "Nothing to it."

"Right," I had said, biting at my dry lips. "I believe it."

I stood there looking first at the tiny sunflower shoots. One wrong step and I'd crush them all. Then I looked at the tree. Murph was hollering, "Put the hammer and nails in your pocket. Good. That's the way."

I took a deep breath and began to inch my way up the trunk, one hand over the other. I couldn't look down. I couldn't swallow.

"That's it," Murph was telling me. "Just a little more."

"I know," I said, but I didn't really. I had no idea what I was going to do when I reached the branch.

Murph knew, though. As I climbed I could see his face more clearly. He was leaning out, grinning at me.

And then I was there in the crook of the branches. Murph was right. It wasn't that high up. I could have jumped down if I had wanted.

Jumped down carefully, I told myself, thinking of Murph's ankle.

I could see what he had started. It was simple really. A couple of boards were nailed against the branches. They were nailed tight enough to make a terrific spot to sit in.

I grabbed one of the nails and began to hammer. "You don't need much force," Murph said. "Just hit it straight."

"And keep my thumb out of the way," I said.

Downstairs I could see Andrew coming out. His face was shiny clean, his hair slicked back. He was wearing a new sweater my mother had knitted.

I was in an interesting spot, I thought. I could see everything that was going on . . . the houses across the way, Mrs. Caluzzi putting flowerpots out on her porch—and two kids coming down the street. It looked as if they were stopping every two seconds to do a *changement*.

Some *changement*. They looked like pretzels.

What two kids? One seemed to be wearing a

frilly skirt. I didn't pay too much attention. I was hammering carefully. One nail was in nice and solid. I started on the next. I could hear Murphy whistling.

Murphy was thrilled. He was going to get his tree house after all.

I crossed my fingers. I had a long way to go.

And I did something else. I thought about ballet. In my head I was Juliet, dancing... dancing.

I blinked. The girl coming down the street did have on a frilly skirt. It looked like something her mother would wear to a dance. Stephanie Witt.

The other one was dressed in a cowgirl outfit. Karen Cooper, of course.

Now they were closer. Stephanie looked up and saw me.

It was a little embarrassing. Here they were looking really great and I...

"Aren't you getting dressed?" Karen asked, shading her eyes as she squinted up. "Miss Elise will be here before supper."

"I have time," I said. "I just have to finish nail-

ing this together. Then I'll get ready."

"Don't bother her," Murph said, halfway out the window. "She's doing a great job."

Just then a car came around the corner. It was long and sleek and shiny black. A limo right here on my street. I stopped hammering.

It was Miss Elise, the artistic director.

She was here. Now. About four hours early.

Chapter 8

Miss Elise turned out to be like everybody else. Almost. She had a little scraggly hair coming out of her bun, and she had a pack of Life Savers in her pocket that she passed around to everyone.

"I love the frilly skirt," she told Stephanie.

"I love the cowgirl outfit," she told Karen.

And then she looked at me. "And that is the greatest looking tree house I ever..."

"Well," I said, "I'm working on it." I had to smile. It really was coming along. I knew it was going to be just what Murph wanted.

Then my mother came outside. Her hair was looking scraggly all over. She still hadn't gotten her bath either.

She saw the limo and Miss Elise and rolled her eyes at me. Miss Elise kept saying she was sorry to be so early, and my mother kept saying it was fine.

In two minutes, my mother had us in the house. Miss Elise still kept saying she was sorry she was so early. We drank iced tea with ice cubes. We munched on my father's special homemade macaroon cookies from two days ago.

And we found out what was different about Miss Elise. She told a million stories about ballet.

"Ballet began in the 1600s," she said. "Groups of dancers made pretty patterns on the stage for kings. They wore long dresses and heels on their slippers."

Miss Elise bit into a macaroon cookie. "Telling a story in dance didn't come until later."

I watched Stephanie grab the last cookie. Karen wasn't eating at all. I could see she was concentrating on her swan neck. Her head was stretched up the way Miss Deirdre liked to see it.

I tried a swan neck, too.

Next we heard about a dancer from Belgium named Marie Camargo. "She lived in the 1700s." Miss Elise popped the rest of her cookie into her mouth. "Marie took the heels off her slippers. She hemmed up her long dress to show her ankles. She wanted everyone to see her beautiful footwork."

And that's the way the next few days went. At breakfast, Miss Elise told me about ballerinas dancing *en pointe*. "Dancing on their toes makes them seem light and airy," she said. "Almost as if they're floating above the stage."

That's all I thought about, ballet. And in between, I practiced and told Miss Elise about my own stuff—cleaning the house and Murph's ankle.

Miss Elise even went to look at the tree house up close, the tree house that I hammered and hammered at, a minute here, a minute there. On the way over, she told me more about *en pointe*. "Not for you yet," she said. "But someday when your feet are really strong, you'll dance on your toes."

"I know," I said. And I really did know.

Tryouts weren't until Thursday. But by Sunday, I felt I'd never be picked, even though I worked on ballet in my room every night, even though I worked again in the mornings. I did *pas de chat* around the dining room table. I did *changements* in the living room, and *soutenus* in the hall.

But Joy Mead was doing the same thing at her house. And Joy was really good. I sighed. Joy was nice. It was hard to want her to lose.

And then the week was flying by. There was no class on Tuesday. On Wednesday, Amy knocked on the back door and invited me to the ballet. "I'm not dancing today," she said. "So we'll watch together in the wings."

"Do it." Miss Elise waved her hand. "I would go with you, but it's my holiday in this yellow castle with Andrew."

I raced up to grab my best jacket. I ran a comb through my hair, whooshed on a spray of my mother's Spring Blossom perfume, and I was ready.

And then we were there. We drove through the city with Amy's father. We got out of the car and went through the back door of the theater.

It was the same as it had been last time. Carpenters were bustling around backstage. They were doing last minute things with the scenery.

A few of the dancers were standing, heads down, eyes closed.

Amy pointed to them. "Sometimes the dancers go over their roles, picturing exactly what they'll do during the performance."

I nodded and looked around, trying to see everything at once. Some of the dancers were already dressed. Their costumes were covered with tiny bits of glass that sparkled every time they moved. But instead of ballet slippers, a few of them still wore socks, old and thick.

"To keep their feet warm," Amy said. "See how they point and stretch. It's important not to get cold while they're waiting. Cold feet make a dancer's movements stiff."

Another dancer was standing at the rosin box. First she stuck the heels of her tights into it. Then she laced on her slippers and stepped into the box again.

"See," Amy pointed, "with rosin on her feet, her slippers will stick better. With rosin on her slippers, she won't slip on the floor."

Then we went toward the dressing rooms. I looked over my shoulder, watching dancers warm up at the barre. I knew from last time they'd pull the barre off the stage just before the curtain went up.

We walked down the hall. I was looking for the Juliet dancer. And there she was, surrounded by jars and tubes of makeup, smiling to see me. "You've come on the best day," she said.

One of her dainty ballet slippers was in her hand. She was sewing ribbons on it. "I have to do this myself," she said. "It has to be absolutely right."

She shivered. "This is my most important day."

I stood there watching as she took quick, tiny stitches. "At last I dance Juliet. Today."

"Wonderful," Amy was saying. And I said it, too.

"It was hard," she said. "There were so many disappointments." She pointed the slipper at me. "I heard that you're practicing, girl in the pink dress. I heard you're working hard."

"I am," I said. "Really." I wondered if it would make any difference. I didn't feel as if I were one bit better.

"Good." The dancer turned her head to one side. "Then what's the matter?"

I raised one shoulder in the air. How did she know what I was thinking?

She reached for the other slipper and pointed it at me. "I'll tell you something," she said. "You have to believe in yourself. You have to say *I can do this with my eyes closed.*"

She leaned forward. Her eyes were ringed with black pencil. "You have to *know* you can do it."

I nodded. "Yes, I guess...." But I didn't have time to finish.

Up on stage, someone was calling, "Beginners, please, onstage." And Amy and I were on our way to watch in the wings. So was everyone else who wasn't dancing yet.

Amy was whispering. "It always happens this way. The first time someone dances a new role everyone watches. They want to cheer her on. They want to give her luck."

And then as the dancer *bouréed* past us and onto the stage, I saw her face. She didn't look worried, she didn't look frightened. She looked as if she couldn't wait to begin to dance.

I watched her dancing. She looked like a feather, light and airy. Everyone around me was saying, "ah," and "yes."

The music was wonderful. It was hard not to dance, too. I took a step back. I tried a *glissade derrière*, a *changement*. And for a few moments, I

was a dancer. I was graceful and strong, and I almost felt as if I could *pas de chat* out onto the stage.

But it was only for those few moments.

Then I thought of the tryouts with Miss Elise.

Tomorrow.

Chapter 9

Miss Elise had gone to Dance with Miss Deirdre ahead of me. I was alone in the kitchen with Grandpa.

He was whistling "Rakes of Mallow." He said it was one of his all-time favorite songs.

I was tucking my pink ballet slippers into my bag, and the good-luck note my mother and father had left me before they went to work. The note that just said, *Love you, Rosie.*

At the last minute, I ran upstairs to get my Juliet puppet. Maybe that would bring me luck.

Karen was banging at the back door. She did a quick *grand battement* while she waited for me.

"This is it," I told Grandpa. I could feel my lips wiggling a little. My hands were wet, and I was tired. I had spent the last hour working on ballet.

Grandpa gave me a hug. "Rosie-Posie, don't worry. If you're not picked, you can spend the summer here. You can clean with me, and hammer up another tree house."

"Stop," I said. "Now I have to win."

"I guess so," he said.

Grandpa went back to whistling, and Karen and I headed for Scranton Avenue. We took a quick stop to look at the tree house and to wave to Murph. I had finished the house just this morning.

"I can't believe you did that," Karen said as we headed for Scranton Avenue and Dance with Miss Deirdre.

"Mr. Murphy helped me finish," I said. I felt great about that tree house. It looked spiffy with the yellow paint. Some of it had dripped down the tree. But even Mr. Murphy said you could hardly see it.

I took a breath. Murph's ankle was better now. And when tryouts were over, we were going to climb up and watch the world.

When tryouts were over. . . . By the time we watched the world, I'd know who had been picked.

In the studio, Miss Serena was at the piano. She was playing music that almost sounded like Grandpa's "Rakes of Mallow." It made me feel better, almost as if Grandpa were there.

Miss Deirdre was talking to Miss Elise, the two of them smiling and nodding. But everyone else looked serious.

I remembered to stay warm, to keep my feet moving and stretching. I squeezed in at the end of the barre.

I thought about Murph. He'd be happy if I hung around with him all summer instead of doing ballet.

I thought about Joy, halfway down the barre. I thought how good she was.

And then we began. I was doing the same things I had been doing for weeks, in my bedroom, in the yard, even on the way home from school.

But it was different.

I could feel Miss Elise's eyes on me.

I moved my feet; I did the *port de bras*. I felt as if my legs were marshmallows, my arms were sticks.

I closed my eyes and listened to the music. I thought of the Juliet dancer and tried to believe in myself. "*Breathe ballet*," I whispered.

The rest of it went a little better, I thought. My *glissade derrière*, the *changement*. By the time I did the *pas de chat* across the center of the studio, I felt fine. It was almost the way it had been yesterday, dancing in back of the stage at the big city ballet. Almost.

And then it was over. I changed out of my slippers and walked home with Miss Elise. She talked about Joy's grace, and Karen's good posture. She talked about Stephanie's smile, and how well I was coming along.

But the one thing she didn't say was who she was going to choose.

And that's the only thing I really wanted to hear.

Chapter 10

It was Friday morning. Miss Elise was leaving. The black limo was at the door again, and Grandpa bumped her suitcase along the front path.

She gave me a hug. "You're a great ballerina," she said as I opened the car door for her.

We stood on the steps waving, the whole family. I didn't cry until the limo turned the corner and Miss Elise was gone.

I hadn't gotten the part. Joy had.

We went back into the kitchen, Andrew tugging at my sleeve. "Don't cry," he kept saying. "You're the princess in this yellow castle."

I tried to smile at him. Then I was crying into

Grandpa's shirt again, and my mother was patting my shoulder.

My father kept shaking his head as he scrambled up a bunch of eggs for us. "An egg with some buttery toast," he said. "You'll feel better in two minutes."

I sat at the table, sipping orange juice. Across the street I could see Murph walking around under his tree, looking up, whistling.

Maybe if I hadn't spent so much time working on the tree house, I could have been practicing ballet.

And the yellow castle.

If I hadn't…

I shook my head. I was glad I had made the tree house. Murph thought it was terrific. And so did I. I wasn't afraid to climb and—

My father slid the plate of eggs in front of me. "See," he said. "She's smiling already."

Grandpa gave me a big plaid handkerchief to wipe my eyes. And my mother said, "Rosie, there will be other chances."

I felt my eyes fill with tears again. "I know."

"The main thing is to keep practicing," my father said.

"And believing in yourself," said Grandpa.

I nodded. Then I took a bite of the scrambled eggs. Delicious. And the buttery toast. Even better.

Andrew was watching me. He looked worried. "I'm all right," I told him.

"I know," he said.

And then I knew it, too. I went over to Murph's to watch him climb to the tree house for the first time. I climbed with him. Then we sat there on the yellow boards, looking at the world.

"Great, isn't it?" he said. He pointed to our sunflowers. They were nice and straight. I could picture how terrific they'd look with flowers next month.

I flexed my feet. "Hello, toes," I whispered, and pulled them closer to my legs. "Good-bye, toes," I said, as I pushed them away.

I was planning again. I was going to work all

summer. I was going to start over.

Across the street, I could hear Amy Stetson's front door fly open and slam shut in back of her.

I leaned over to get a better look. Amy was dashing across the street, waving her arms at us. "Do you think there's room for me up there?" she asked.

I would have said no, but Mr. Murphy had added a thousand nails. "Strong as an ox," he had told me.

"Come on up," Murph said.

A moment later, Amy was sitting beside us in about an inch of room. I wanted to tell her about Miss Elise and not winning, but I didn't have a chance.

She knew it already. "Your grandpa told me," she said. "But guess what? It doesn't make any difference."

I didn't say anything. I just bit my lip.

Amy smiled at me. "Want to know what Juliet said?"

"You told…" I began.

Amy nodded. "She said it happened to her. It happens to everyone. Sometimes someone else is better. Sometimes it's just luck. You have to keep working."

"Really?" I asked. "It happened to Juliet?"

Amy kept nodding. "And she said..."

It happened to Juliet. My mother was right. It wasn't the worst thing.

Amy tapped my arm. "Everyone saw you dancing."

"Dancing?"

"In back of the stage."

I felt my face get red. "I didn't know that."

Amy kept smiling. "They said you were graceful and strong. They want you to come to the city this summer. Every day. You can practice with us, and watch the dancers."

I couldn't believe it. "It's as good as..." I began.

"Yes, it is," Amy said. "Every bit as good, because they want you to hold the basket of flowers onstage. You'll replace the girl who moved away."

I closed my eyes. I could feel the syrup of happiness in my chest. I loved the yellow tree house. I loved the yellow castle across the street, and Grandpa and ...

Murphy was grinning at me.

... and Amy, and Murphy, and the sunflowers.

And someday I was going to be a ballerina like Juliet.

From Rosie's Notebook

Artistic director   The person who decides which ballet to perform and chooses the dancers for the roles.

Barre ("BAR")   It's a handrail in front of a mirror. Hold on and warm up!

Bourée ("boo-RAY")   Tiny traveling steps.

Corps de ballet ("COR de bal-LAY")   A large group of dancers who dance together.

Changement ("shanj-MA")   With your legs crossed, jump starting with one foot in front and landing with the other in front.

Demi-seconde ("DEH-me se-KOHN")   An arm position halfway between the first position, where the arms are at your sides, and second position, where your arms are straight out at the shoulders.

En haut ("ahn OAT")   Arm *en haut* means hold your arms above your head.

En pointe ("ahn PWAN")   Dancing on the tips of your toes, wearing toe shoes.

First position   Place your heels together. Turn your feet and legs to the sides.

Glissade derrière ("gli-SAHD deh-ree-AIR")   I love the way this looks. It's a traveling step. Start off with the heel of your right foot in front of the middle of the left. Lean your head to the side. Slide your left foot out, and begin to raise your arms over your head. Raise your left foot, point, then spring. As you land on your left foot, stretch your right foot off the ground. (Find a picture. It's not as hard as it sounds!)

Grand battement ("GRON baht-MA") Start in fifth position, right foot in front. Then throw your leg up through fourth position into the air, and back down again, keeping both knees straight.

Jeté ("zheh-TAY") This is a jump from one foot to another.

Mime ("MYM") Acting out feelings or a story without words.

Open fourth One foot is directly forward from first position by about a foot. Remember to keep your feet turned out.

Pas de chat ("pa de SHAH") This means the "step of a cat." Jump with your knees bent, right foot first. Land on your right foot and close the left.

Plié ("plee-AY") In any of the positions, slowly bend and then straighten your knees.

Pirouette ("peer-oo-ET") The ballerina is up on one toe. Her other foot is pointed in back of her knee. Sometimes she turns alone. Sometimes her partner supports her.

Port de bras ("POR de BRA") These are arm movements going from one position to the other. Doing these exercises teaches you to move your arms gracefully.

Rosin ("ROZ-in") A dry, sticky substance made from pine tree sap. Dancers use it to coat the bottom of their slippers. They don't want to slip during a performance.

Soutenu ("SOO-ten-oo") A turning step.

Understudy This person studies a part to be ready to dance instead of the principal dancer, if it is necessary.

PATRICIA REILLY GIFF is the author of more than fifty books for young readers, including the popular Ronald Morgan books, the best-selling *Kids of the Polk Street School* series, the Newbery Honor Book *Lily's Crossing*, and many works of nonfiction.

A former teacher and reading consultant, Ms. Giff lives in Weston, Connecticut.

JULIE DURRELL has illustrated more than thirty books for children. She lives in Cambridge, Massachusetts.